Praise for
SUSAN SHREVE'S
Jonah the Whale and How He Became Incredibly Famous

"Susan Shreve writes with snap and verve; it's a treat to see a young hero so ably making lemonade out of an acid bath."

—*The New York Times Book Review*

"Susan Shreve has a spectacular gift for taking ordinary youngsters and making them do extraordinary things. And she does it with a light, ironic touch."

—*Philadelphia Enquirer*

"Middle schoolers, especially those feeling a bit out of step, will cheer when Jonah actually pulls off this nearly impossible feat."

—*Publishers Weekly*

"Shreve works magic with her writing making Jonah's story perfectly plausible."

—*The Washington Post Book World*

"Shreve's understatement and restraint lend a solidity to the kid-success story that such plots rarely possess."

—*Bulletin of the Center for Children's Books*

"Jonah is an appealing hero with believable motivations, a loving but beleaguered mother, and a refreshingly sassy friend in Blister."

—*Booklist*

Jonah the Whale
and how
he became
INCREDIBLY
FAMOUS

a novel by

Susan Shreve

Previously published as
Jonah, the Whale

SCHOLASTIC
Signature

an imprint of
Scholastic Inc.

New York   Toronto   London   Auckland   Sydney
Mexico City   New Delhi   Hong Kong

ISBN 0-439-22849-2   Library of Congress number 97-10785

12 11 10 9 8 7 6 5 4 3   1 2 3 4 5/0

Printed in the U.S.A.   40

First Scholastic paperback printing, September 2000

Previously published as *Jonah, the Whale*
First Scholastic paperback printing, February 1999

Original hardcover edition designed by Elizabeth Parisi,
published by Arthur A. Levine Books, an imprint of Scholastic Press, May 1998.

Welcome
Emmett Adams Seldes Carnahan
August 14, 1997

■ CONTENTS ■

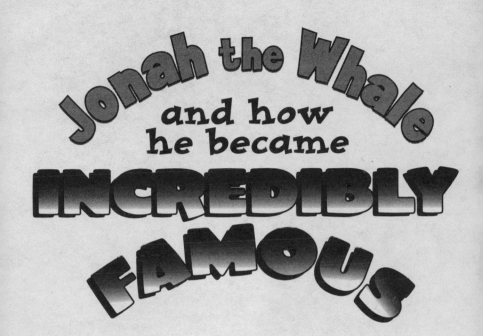

Jonah the Whale
and how
he became
INCREDIBLY
FAMOUS

■ THE BEGINNING ■

O N E

Jonah stood at the window of his new bedroom, looking down over a courtyard of children he didn't know, had never even met. They were on their way to school, spilling out of the brown-brick apartment complex in Springwood where he'd lived for eleven days and twelve nights after Thomas Hale, his mother's boyfriend, the only father he had ever known, had disappeared in New York City — Jonah's home, the place where he was born.

Thomas Hale was not a subject he was permitted to bring up.

"You need to know just this," his mother had told him the night before at dinner. "The name Thomas Hale is canceled in our house."

"Where do you think he's gone to?" Jonah asked quietly.

"Now, do you think I care where he's gone to?" his mother said, piling more spaghetti on his plate. "Paris, Nigeria, the Bronx. He could be anyplace. It's a big world." She sat down in front of her empty plate. Recently she had not been eating. "All I know is, he's not here."

Later, when Jonah was reading to his baby brother Quentin, his mother had come into his room in a sweet mood and patted his head.

"It's on you now, baby," she had said. "I'm counting that you'll be somebody so you can take care of your little family."

All night Jonah had tossed and turned, thinking of what he — an oversized eleven-year-old boy, called good-looking only by his grandmother — could do to take care of his little family. He was an okay student according to his teachers, but not athletic; there wasn't much to recommend him as a new sixth grader at Bixley Elementary. Except his imagination. Everyone who knew Jonah Morrison knew about that.

"You cannot tell the truth without making it bigger than it is, Jonah," his mother would say, shaking her head in frustration. "Bigger than any truth could ever be."

Thomas Hale had disagreed.

"Your imagination is a good thing, Jonah," he'd said just before he left. "It could take you someplace."

Lying in his new bedroom at the Bixley Apartments, no curtains on the window, only a half-moon perfectly drawn on the sky, Jonah decided to make sure his family could count on him. He could be famous.

And then his almost-father, wherever he was living, would read about Jonah Morrison in *People* magazine and recognize him and come home. *People* was Thomas's favorite magazine. He read every issue cover to cover.

In the kitchen, his mother was in a hurry.

"Eat up," she said to Quentin, who was picking up his Cheerios one by one, stuffing them in his tiny mouth. "We've got to hurry. I can't be late for work."

Work for Nora Morrison was at the high-school cafeteria in North Haven. Every morning, she and Jonah left together. He walked to Bixley Elementary and she took Quentin on a bus, dropped him at day care, and went on to North Haven arriving at nine A.M. In the afternoon, after school, Jonah took a bus to the day-care center to pick up Quentin and take him back to the Bixley apartment complex, where they waited for their mother to get home from her second job, at seven-thirty.

In New York City, Jonah's mother had had a job at his own school cafeteria, and Thomas Hale stayed home with Quentin during the day and worked nights. Sometimes Jonah and his mother walked home together, and in the evenings, she was always the one to take care of Quentin while Thomas was at work. Now she had to work too many hours and there was no father to help out, so Quentin was Jonah's responsibility.

"Are you ready for school, Jonah?" his mother called from the kitchen.

"Just about," Jonah said.

Which wasn't quite true.

He owned three pairs of pants — one pair of blue jeans, two corduroys — bought this summer when they'd had enough money for extras, and already they were too tight. Now they lay on the floor, where he had tossed them after he tried them on.

His mother came to the door.

"Can you tell me why you're standing there in your underpants at seven-thirty in the morning, when we are supposed to be walking out the door?" she asked.

He turned his head away, folded his arms across his chest.

"My pants have gotten too tight."

"These new pants we got in August?" his mother asked, picking up the brown corduroys from the floor. "That's not a possibility. Here. Try these on."

Jonah did, pulling the trousers up, dragging them over his hips, trying to snap the button at the waist.

"See?"

"Well, sweetheart, they'll just have to do." She took a sweater out of his drawer and handed it to him. "Keep this on so you can cover up your belly."

It wasn't cold enough for a sweater, but Jonah put it on and pulled it down over his stomach.

"You're hungry all the time," his mother said, putting on Quentin's jacket, buttoning it up under his chin. "Eating enough for you and Thomas won't bring him back, Jonah."

Jonah shrugged. He had been hungry, all right. Starving, as if there were a hole the size of a volcano in the center of him and he had to keep filling it or he would erupt. He asked for seconds and thirds at lunch and at dinner. On the way home with Quentin from the day-care center, he stopped at Sweets 'n' Things and got a double-decker ice-cream cone for a snack: chocolate and chocolate swirl. If his mother had bought graham crackers at the supermarket, he could eat the whole box before she got home from work. And he was still hungry when he went to bed at night, dreaming of his grandmother's sweet-potato pie.

He followed his mother down the steps of the court-yard. He didn't like to walk with his mother and Quentin out of the Bixley apartment complex into that crowd of strangers his age, who had already been good friends for years. His mother always made a fuss kissing him good-bye, telling him to mind his manners and not talk too much in class — as if there were a chance in the world that he'd talk at all. Besides, he couldn't talk. His pants were so tight, he felt as if he were walking in a stiff carton without any room to breathe.

He walked alone to school. No one bothered to speak to him or ask him to join their group or invite him to do something at recess. But Jonah was used to that. He'd spent a lot of time alone. In New York City, he had changed schools twice. Once when they moved from his grandmother's apartment in Brooklyn, and another time when Thomas lost his janitor's job at Columbia University and they'd moved from 108th Street to the East Village.

In his first week in Springwood, Jonah had learned if he walked one block east and then turned north on Greeley Street, he could arrive at Bixley Elementary the back way and not have to travel conspicuously — one lone boy in the middle of a crowd.

So he walked that way today. At the corner of Greeley and Sagamore, he saw a girl from his class whom he had noticed because her hair was very red, her face plastered with freckles, and she had the peculiar name of Blister. She was walking alone and Jonah fell into step with her.

"You probably don't like Bixley because the kids here are sort of meaner than kids in other places," Blister said to him, swinging her backpack off her shoulder, walking with her head forward, not looking at him.

He liked the way she looked. She was a small girl, with long legs and tiny white hands and a turned-up nose. Today she had lavender nail polish on her fingernails, which she showed to Jonah.

"I put this stuff on to be cool," she said. "That's what my sister told me I should do, since the kids in sixth grade don't pay any attention to me or invite me for sleep-overs."

"It's nice," Jonah said. "Really purple."

"I know," Blister said. "It's called Purple Rain. My sister is married."

"I have a sister who's married, too," Jonah said, lying easily. He didn't even have a sister. It just suddenly seemed like a good thing to have one and so he decided to have one. Besides, he liked Blister and wanted to have something in common with her.

"The thing about Bixley is that a lot of the kids are poor like us, and they don't have fathers like me, and they depend on each other to be their family," Blister said. "That's what my sister told me and that's why it's hard to make friends." She looked over at Jonah. "Do you have a father?"

Jonah hesitated. He hadn't told anyone about Thomas. Not the kids at his school in the East Village, which he'd left in mid-September, and certainly not the kids at Bixley.

"I do have a father," Jonah said. "Thomas. He's traveling in Africa now, helping the poor."

"That's cool," Blister said.

"Yeah," Jonah said. "He's a great man."

"My father's married to someone called Trixie. We don't like her. Especially me."

They had come to the back of Bixley Elementary, and Blister stopped.

"You don't think I'll be in trouble for this nail polish, do you?" she asked.

"I don't know," Jonah said. "I don't know the rules at Bixley."

Blister shrugged. "Well, if I do get in trouble, I'll just run away from home."

And then she saw another girl in the sixth grade named Anne coming around the side of the building. She waved wildly, called good-bye to Jonah, and ran up the steps, showing off her nail polish.

So Jonah ended up walking into the school building alone after all. It was Monday, his sixth day of Bixley Elementary — and so far, in one full week, he had no friends at all, unless he could call Blister one. Kids hadn't been unkind to him — not directly, not to his face. In fact, on his first day of school, the teacher had written on the chalkboard: **Bixley Sixth Grade Welcomes Jonah Morrison.** But he had the feeling that when he walked away or into the cafeteria or out the front door after school, they were laughing or making fun of the way he walked or the way he talked or the way he looked from behind. He had a hollowed-out feeling of homesickness all the time, even though home was only half a mile away.

He opened his locker, hung up his jacket and book bag, took out his library book, and walked down the corridor into Mr. Parker's sixth-grade classroom.

It was too early for the bell, and Mr. Parker had not arrived yet. Several students were standing around, talking and laughing, their arms thrown over one another's shoulders, and a few were doing their homework from the night before.

When Jonah walked into the room, there was a change like the weather. He sat down in his assigned seat, front row, right, near the window, and opened his library book so he could appear to be busy — but he had an uncomfortable sense that something was different about this morning, somehow wrong.

Only then did he look up and notice the chalkboard. Written in big letters with yellow chalk, under the date and homework for the first week of October, was the message:

Bixley Sixth Grade Welcomes Jonah, the Whale.

T W O

onah didn't react. He was good at that. He knew how to pretend that he was perfectly fine even when he wasn't.

"You'd make a good actor, Jonah," his grandmother would say to him. "You pull the wool over my eyes every time."

He was a good actor. No one would ever guess what Jonah Morrison was thinking — except maybe his mother, and lately she had been too busy with other things to take him into account.

When the bell rang, he walked to science class, past the library, down the corridor past the assembly room, past the fifth-grade classrooms, into Ms. Pepper's science class. He sat down at a table next to Blister.

She leaned over. "See what I was saying?" Blister whispered. "I don't know who wrote 'Jonah, the Whale' on the blackboard. Probably some mean, mean boy I'd like to exterminate."

He nodded blankly, pulling at the waistband of his jeans, which squeezed his middle.

■   ■   ■

In science, the sixth grade was studying insects. Ms. Pepper, a small woman with blazing eyes and a lisp that made her sound like a child, handed out a laminated sheet with pictures of familiar insects.

"I'm sure you've seen roaches before," she said. "They are in all the apartments in Springwood that I've been in."

The roaches reminded Jonah of New York — particularly of the East Village apartment — where small brown leggy roaches invaded the kitchen at night. After dark, if Jonah went into the kitchen and turned on the lights, the linoleum counters would be full of them: busy, fast-moving insects, extremely ugly, full of aggressive confidence, and fearless. He hated them.

The night before Thomas Hale had left in September, Jonah heard him in the kitchen opening and shutting drawers.

Jonah found Thomas in his undershorts, emptying out the cupboards.

"What are you looking for?" he asked.

"Poison," Thomas said.

"Poison?"

"I'm looking to kill these roaches," he said. "They keep me awake at night."

Jonah had slipped into a chair at the small kitchen table in the corner beside the fridge.

"How come you can hear them?" he asked.

"I know they're here running around, so I hear them," Thomas said.

Thomas Hale was a tall man, a little skinny, with big legs and glasses he wore tipped on the end of his nose unless he was reading. When he was young, he'd been an athlete. He still looked like an athlete, a little over the hill. He'd been a basketball player. In the hall closet, there were hundreds of pictures in a cardboard box, even newspaper articles about his playing. For two years running, he had been the high scorer, All-City, and in the box were trophies from those years.

Then he went to college on a basketball scholarship, got bad grades, got in trouble with his professors, and dropped out after a year.

"Thomas Hale could have been something else," Jonah's mother had told him. "But he quit."

His mother had been the one to show Jonah the pictures, because Thomas never mentioned anything he'd done. Not his sports, not his jobs, not his college career. He was not a conversational man.

But there was a conversation he liked to have with Jonah.

On days when Thomas's temper was bad, Jonah knew

he could cheer him up by talking about famous people. He found his famous people in *People* magazine. It was a magazine about celebrities and also ordinary people who had extraordinary lives. Every week Thomas Hale would buy the latest edition at the supermarket and pore over the stories at the kitchen table. Jonah liked to sit at the table with him.

"So, who do you like this week?" Jonah would ask, watching him cut out one story or another to put in the manila folder where he kept his favorites.

Thomas liked the stories about people who had done something unusual with their lives.

"I like a man who makes up his life. Who comes from nothing, and gets an idea like driving around in an ice-cream truck or inventing a three-wheeler bike or a video camera or a baby doll that wets. That's the kind of man I'd like to be."

"No chance you're going to be that kind of man," his mother said. "Not unless you get out of your chair and stop reading magazines about people who do something, and go do something yourself."

Jonah loved his mother, but she was hard on Thomas — especially after he was fired from Columbia University and couldn't seem to get another job.

That last night with Thomas, Jonah sat in the kitchen and watched him wash away the roaches when he couldn't find any poison. He took a sponge and pushed them into the sink and turned the faucet on, watching them plunge down the drain to their deaths. And when he had finished, he sat down at the table with Jonah and opened up a beer.

"Are they gone for good?" Jonah asked.

"For good? Not a chance," Thomas had said. "They'll be back tomorrow night."

"So you'll have to do it again tomorrow night?" Jonah asked.

"I don't think so, Jonah," Thomas had said. "I think I'm done killing roaches."

They moved to Springwood because his aunt Lavinia lived there and Lavinia was his mother's favorite sister. "A good-time girl," Lavinia called herself, plump and saucy.

"Besides," his mother had said, "I can't afford to live in New York City without a man."

"He may come back," Jonah said.

"If he has in mind coming back, he'll find us in Springwood," she said.

But Jonah didn't want to leave. Thomas knew where they were in New York, and he might not be able to find them if they moved.

"Can we leave a message on the door?" he'd asked his mother when they had packed up to leave.

"What kind of good will that do, Jonah?" she asked. "New people are going to be moving in here when we go, and they don't want a message on their door."

But Jonah wrote a message anyway, and left it on the door when his mother wasn't looking.

Dear Thomas,
      We have moved to Springwood, near New Haven,
which is less expensive than New York. We live at the
Bixley Apartments. Probably we'll have a phone soon.
                  Love from your friends,
                  Jonah and Quentin

At recess, Jonah asked for permission to go to the library and read. He didn't want to stand on the playground by himself. It embarrassed him not to have friends. When they had lived near Columbia University, he had a friend called Karl Slatov — every day, they walked to school together. There'd been other friends uptown he could count on to play with, so he never had to stand on the playground alone during recess. Later, down in the East Village, he'd had a reputation for being smart and telling crazy stories. Even though he didn't have good friends at P.S. 146, he was someone important. The other kids knew who he was when they passed him on the street and always spoke to him.

Now he sat down at the library table and opened *The Adventures of Huckleberry Finn.*

"I want to show them I am somebody," he remembered Thomas saying to his mother sometime this past summer.

"Show who?" his mother had asked.

"The world, Nora," Thomas had said. "Anybody who'll pay attention."

Mr. Parker came into the library and sat down at the table next to Jonah and asked if he was making friends.

"Sure," Jonah said. "I have some friends, but I haven't gotten to know them too well yet."

"It can be difficult to move to a new school," Mr. Parker said.

"I know," Jonah said. "This isn't the first time I've moved."

"I am sorry about the message on the board," Mr. Parker told him. "We have some boys who can be unkind, and I hope it didn't hurt your feelings."

"It didn't hurt my feelings," Jonah said.

He certainly wasn't going to let Mr. Parker know that he was worried or sad. In fact, he didn't want Mr. Parker to know anything about him at all.

He sat with Blister and her friend Anne at lunch, and was glad of that, glad to have a temporary friend so he didn't have to sit alone — even if she was a girl with Purple Rain on her nails. Anne kept her head down and ate her ravioli, but Blister was a talker.

"It's kind of weird to sit with you at lunch," she said. "I mean, I never sit with a boy, because the sixth-grade boys wouldn't dare to sit with me."

"How come?" Jonah asked.

"Because I'm a girl, I guess," Blister said. "And sitting with you is a little risky, since I can tell you aren't too popular. I know about that because when I moved here after my father married Trixie, I wasn't popular, either." She opened her carton of chocolate milk. "I'm still not popular, because Anne's the only person who asked me to her birthday party so far this year."

"I didn't ask you," Anne said. "You asked yourself."

"But you should do sports, Jonah," Blister went on, ignoring Anne. "If you want to be popular, that's the thing for a boy to do." She drank her milk straight down without stopping. "Right, Anne?"

Anne nodded.

"Like now, you should try out for the soccer team," Blister said.

"I can't," Jonah said, shrugging.

"'Cause you're fat?" Blister asked.

"Not really. I'm just not any good at sports," Jonah said. "I mean, I know I'm fat, but that's not why I'm bad at sports."

Somehow Blister didn't hurt his feelings. It was as though she said what she saw and that was that. Besides, he could tell she liked him.

"I didn't used to be fat," Jonah said. "When we moved here, I started to get hungry all the time."

"I know what you mean," Blister said.

"Even when I was skinny, I couldn't do sports at all,"

Jonah said. "My father was a great basketball player. All-City in New York. But I'm more like my mother."

"Me, too," Blister said sadly. "And my mother is a pain in the neck."

During social studies, Jonah sat in the back of the class. His mind drifted from the study of South America to the *People* magazines Thomas read every week.

Something came to him, floating by like a scent, a half-formed muddy thought that he couldn't quite grab out of the air and hold. He opened his notebook and began a letter to Thomas.

Dear Thomas,

I thought you would like to know that I am planning to go into television soon. I am developing my own show. I think you will like it.

Things are going well here. We have a wonderful apartment with four bedrooms and a picture window overlooking a park, and a maid who helps out with Quentin, especially since I am working on my television program. Mama looks very beautiful. She got some new clothes with the money from her job and is very foxy. You'd be surprised. We don't have a telephone yet, but I'll send you the number soon.

Love from your friend,
Jonah Morrison

P.S. The television show is called Jonah, the Whale. *Today when I walked into homeroom at Bixley, someone had written "Jonah, the Whale" on the blackboard. I guess it's because I've gotten a little fat since you left. But I remember the things you told me and so I thought, I'll show them. Jonah, the Whale, will be somebody.*

THREE

Quentin had a cold. When Jonah picked him up at day care, the director called him aside.

"We have to be careful about the other children," she said. "You tell your mother not to bring Quentin to day care if he has a cold."

"My mother has to go to work," Jonah said.

"But I have to protect my other children," the director said. "You understand that, don't you?"

Of course, Jonah understood. He wasn't an idiot, but he wouldn't give the director the satisfaction of his apology, either. Didn't she know that Thomas Hale had left without an announcement, that the Morrisons were strangers to Springwood and didn't have friends except Aunt Lavinia, and that the sixth graders at Bixley Elementary had been unkind to Jonah? Didn't she know anything?

He picked up Quentin, who was very glad to see him — wrapping his short plump arms around his brother's neck while Jonah tried to dress him in his jacket and hat.

"We probably won't be back," Jonah said under his

breath to the director as they were leaving, but she didn't seem to hear him.

On the way to the bus stop, Jonah thought about the television show that had been slipping around his mind since school. A television show for children was what he had in mind. Children-to-children — about amazing people, like some of the ones described in *People* magazine. But he needed to do a study of television first, and the Morrisons didn't own a TV. So he stopped at a public telephone on Hawthorne Street and called Aunt Lavinia, who happened to be at home. Most days Aunt Lavinia worked in the hospital, pulling blood out of people's veins in those long needles and sending it to the laboratory for examination. Jonah didn't even like to think about her job.

"I was wondering if Quentin and I could come over and watch television for a homework assignment I have," he asked his aunt.

"Tell the teacher you can't be doing assignments that require a television, if you don't have any to look at except mine," she told him.

"I don't want him to know we can't afford one," Jonah said.

"That's not the point, sweetheart," Aunt Lavinia said. "Your mama doesn't want you to wear your brain out watching TV."

"So are you saying I can't come over and watch your television?" Jonah asked.

"Of course not," Aunt Lavinia said. "I'm telling you what I'm telling you. But if you've got to be watching television for homework you'd better beat it over here."

"I'll be there soon," Jonah said. He decided not to tell Aunt Lavinia about Quentin's cold.

At Hawthorne he got on the L4 to Darcy; and then took the Crosstown to Harcom Lane and 16th.

Quentin was fussy on the bus. The woman sitting in the seat in front of Jonah asked if he couldn't keep his baby quiet, since she had a headache. Another woman stopped at his seat just before she got off the bus and said, "With a cough like that, that baby could have pneumonia."

"He doesn't have pneumonia," Jonah said, looking directly at the woman. "He's allergic to Springwood."

Jonah was beginning to think he might move back to New York City on his own. The people here were too bad-tempered.

There was a newsstand where he got off the bus at the corner of Harcom Lane and 16th. He stopped to get a copy of *People* magazine, stuffing it into his book bag so that Aunt Lavinia wouldn't see it and wonder.

"Ice cream," Quentin said, burrowing his head in Jonah's neck.

"I don't see an ice-cream place, Quentin," Jonah said.

"I want ice cream," Quentin insisted, his nose running, his eyes puffy.

"We're going to Aunt Lavinia's," Jonah said. "Maybe she has ice cream."

But Aunt Lavinia didn't have ice cream. Or cookies or juice or graham crackers or pretzels or anything at all, except a half-eaten carton of lemon yogurt, a bottle of iced tea, and a box of peanut brittle that she was giving as a gift that night and couldn't open.

"I'm sorry, Quentin baby," Aunt Lavinia said. "All I've got for children is a television and a warm lap."

So Quentin climbed into her warm lap and fell asleep, and Jonah turned on the television.

He wanted to look at the kinds of shows on afternoon television. He had a picture in his mind of a large black whale with its mouth open. That's how the show would start, with music playing: *Row, row, row your boat, gently down the stream — merrily, merrily, merrily, merrily — life is but a dream* . . .

In the belly of the whale, visible for all to see, would be Jonah.

"Good afternoon. This is Jonah Morrison, coming to you from my office in the belly of a whale."

And then the camera would zoom in on Jonah and there he'd be, sitting at his desk in the whale's belly, in front of a microphone, dressed in blue jeans — because although he was famous as a newscaster for children all over America, he was still an ordinary boy like all of them.

He liked the idea of broadcasting a television show from a whale. Kids would be pleased by that. It was just the kind of thing they would love.

"Yuck!" they'd say. "There's Jonah again in a whale's tummy. I wonder why he isn't all bloody."

Unfortunately, he wouldn't be able to allow the sixth graders at Bixley Elementary to appear on the show because none of them was exceptional. Except Blister. Maybe Blister could work with him.

As Jonah sat on Aunt Lavinia's couch, surfing the programs on late afternoon television, the future was growing in his mind.

There he was on the set of a television studio, constructed to look like the inside of a whale — he'd seen pictures from the Bible story and *Pinocchio* — he could imagine the inside of a whale. And he'd make a call from his desk, maybe to Madonna. "Hello, Madonna," he'd say. "This is Jonah Morrison, calling from my office at WKBY in the belly of a whale. Are you there, Madonna?"

Lavinia drove them home at seven o'clock in her new, bright-blue Toyota with the music playing low.

"I guess you get a lot of money putting needles in

people," Jonah said as he fastened his seat belt and settled in the front seat. In the back Quentin was complaining.

"I just don't have any babies like your mama does, so all the money I get goes to me," Lavinia said. "That's why I've got a new car."

"So how much money do you think a television producer would get?" Jonah asked.

"A television producer? Now, darling, how would I know that?" Lavinia asked. "I wouldn't know a television producer if I tripped over him on the bus."

"But how much would you guess? A lot?"

"I'd say a lot," Lavinia said, turning the music off. "More than I get at the hospital — and certainly more than your mother gets, serving food at the high school."

"That's what I thought," Jonah said. "Millions is what I thought."

Although millions was more than he could imagine. One hundred dollars would be enough. That was more than he'd ever dreamed of. Aunt Lavinia pulled up to the entrance of the Bixley apartment complex. "Don't speak to strangers," she said, letting Jonah and Quentin out.

"I won't," Jonah said, but he couldn't say any more because Quentin was screaming *"Ice cream!"* at the top of his lungs.

On the stairs going up to the apartment, he met his mother carrying groceries. She looked very tired.

"Hi, sweetheart," she said, kissing his cheek. "Quentin doesn't seem very happy tonight."

"He's sick," Jonah said.

His mother felt Quentin's head.

"The day-care lady said he was too sick to go to day care," Jonah said.

"She should have called me at work. I would have picked him up," his mother said. "She has my number there. It's not her business to tell my son."

"I know," Jonah said, peering in the grocery bag. "I'm starved."

"We're having sweet potato pie just for you," his mother said.

"Thanks, Mama," Jonah said, kissing her shoulder.

He unlocked the door to the apartment, turned on the light, and put Quentin down on the couch.

"I have a lot of homework," he said. "Tons more than in New York."

"Already?" his mother asked as she put away the groceries. "So maybe you like this new school?"

Jonah considered.

"I like it quite a bit," he said.

His mother didn't need to hear bad news, so he wasn't going to tell her. Besides, soon — maybe in a matter of weeks — Jonah Morrison would be so famous that it wouldn't make any difference whether he liked Bixley Elementary or not.

■ ■ ■

He closed the door to his bedroom, turned on the light beside his bed, and opened his backpack. He did have a page of mathematics homework in beginning algebra that he didn't understand, and a composition on the meaning of the word "fall" (as in autumn), and half a page of Spanish vocabulary words to memorize.

But he wasn't thinking about homework. He lay down on his stomach, took out *People* magazine, and opened it to the first page.

F O U R

On Tuesday Jonah didn't go to school. He had stayed up very late reading *People* magazine and clipping out the stories Thomas might have liked. And thinking.

Besides, he couldn't go to school. He hadn't done a bit of homework and doubted that he would have the time in his new profession as a television anchor to do his homework all year.

But he got dressed as if he were going to school, packed his book bag, and sat down to breakfast with his mother, who was still in her bathrobe.

"I'm not going to work today," she said, looking off into the middle distance. "Quentin's still sick and the day-care center won't take him, like you said. So I'm going to the clinic to get some medicine."

"Does that mean you'll be fired?" Jonah asked.

He knew about firing. Thomas had been fired from Columbia University for missing too much work the winter his asthma kicked up, and that had been the beginning of the Morrison family's troubles.

"If I'm fired for taking care of my baby, then I'm fired," his mother said, clearing the table. "You have to make your choices."

"What will we do then?" Jonah asked, pouring himself a second bowl of cereal.

"Either I'll get another job or we'll move in with Aunt Lavinia." His mother closed the box of cereal and put it back in the cupboard. "Now don't eat so much cereal, darling, or you'll explode."

She kissed him good-bye. Jonah put on his jacket and slung his book bag over one shoulder.

Just before he left, he looked out the window in the kitchen, checking the tons of kids on their way to school.

"Don't worry, Jonah," his mother said softly, pulling his baseball cap down over his forehead. "You'll have friends soon enough."

"I'm not worried. I have a friend named Blister already," Jonah said. He walked out the door and down the cement steps into the courtyard of the apartment complex.

His plan was to go downtown on the L4 to Angel Street, where the television station, WKBY, was located. He'd looked it up in the telephone book.

He would ask to speak with the manager. And when the manager invited him in, he planned to say, "I have a television program for you to do for children. By children and for children — and I will be the anchor."

He'd particularly liked two stories in *People* magazine. He'd cut them out and stuffed them in his bookbag to take to WKBY. In one story, a boy about his age in San Francisco had met a homeless man sleeping on the street beside an ice-cream store. The boy had been so struck by the man's terrible situation that, with his parents, he started a program called Food for All, which now fed over a thousand people every night. The second story was about a girl who'd lost both her legs in a car accident and had then become a gymnast, using only her arms. He'd also cut out a story about Michael Jordan, the great basketball player — the article was about his friendship with his father when he was a boy. Michael Jordan was Thomas Hale's favorite athlete in the world. His idol.

In the courtyard of the Bixley Apartments, Jonah saw Max, a small tank of a boy from the sixth grade.

"You're on your way to school? Right?" Max asked, walking with a group of boys that Jonah didn't know.

"I guess," Jonah said. He wasn't going to say "No," of course, although he wasn't on his way to school at all.

They fell into step with him.

"So you're getting to be friends with Blister," Max said.

"Blister's nice," Jonah said.

He could tell that Max was the kind of kid who'd have a few bad things to say about Blister.

"'Nice' isn't what I'd call Blister," Max went on. "Would you, Jason?"

"Blister's got a reputation," one of the other boys said. "I'd steer clear of her, especially since you're new and don't want to get tied up with someone bad."

"What kind of reputation?" Jonah asked.

The boys exchanged glances.

"She has kissed a ton of guys," Max said. "And more than that," he added, with a wicked look.

"Well, she hasn't kissed me," Jonah said.

Which was exactly the wrong thing to say. Max and his friends fell out laughing.

"I guess she hasn't!" Max said.

"She has *some* standards," Jason said.

Jonah shrugged.

If he'd been tall and strong, he would have liked to put his fist under their chins and send them flying above the trees to Mount Kilimanjaro. Instead, he pretended to misunderstand what they'd said about Blister. Turning east onto Greeley Street, he told them good-bye.

Just as the L4 bus to Angel Street came up, he saw Blister turn the corner walking toward him, waving.

"Where are you going?" Blister shouted, hurrying to catch up.

"I have an appointment downtown," Jonah said.

"A doctor's appointment?" she asked.

"A business appointment," he told her.

And the bus doors closed behind him.

He was glad he had seen Blister. At least she would defend him when Max told Mr. Parker that he'd seen Jonah on his way to school and had no idea why he wasn't there. That he'd probably skipped school and was playing hooky.

Soon enough the sixth grade at Bixley would know about Jonah Morrison. And they'd be very sorry they had ever made fun of him.

The bus was crowded, but Jonah slipped between two women in the very back and settled in the seat, daydreaming. He saw himself in his suit, the one his mother had bought him for Aunt Bess's funeral. He was thin and his hair was cut shorter than it was now — like Max's in a buzz cut.

"Hello," he was saying. "This is Jonah Morrison, speaking to you from the White House. I'm about to interview the President of the United States and his daughter, Chelsea, on the subject of American schools. Please stand by."

Music announces the arrival of the President. Jonah steps forward, giving a little bow, and shakes the President's hand. "It's nice to meet you, Mr. President," he says. He shakes hands with Chelsea. "I like your dress," he says. And they sit down on couches in the living room of the White House for a conversation about schools.

Just when he began to imagine his interview with the Spice Girls the bus driver announced Angel Street.

WKBY was located in a small yellow-brick building with an entrance to the side. Inside, a young man at a desk asked Jonah to sign in. Just his name and the time of his arrival.

"Who're you here to see?" the young man asked.

"The manager," Jonah said, matter-of-factly.

The man pointed to the elevator.

"Third floor," he said.

Jonah got in the elevator and pressed 3.

This is going to be easy, he thought.

When the doors opened on the third floor, he saw a young woman with peach-colored hair tied in a bright green ribbon. She was sitting at the reception desk, reading the newspaper, and eating a sticky bun.

"Yes?" she said, not looking up from her newspaper.

"I'm Jonah Morrison."

"Does your mother work here?"

"No, she works in a school cafeteria," Jonah said. "I've come to talk to the manager about a television program."

"Which program?" the woman asked.

"One that I'm doing myself," Jonah said. "Interviews . . ."

"Oh, I see," the woman said. "*You're* doing a television program. Have you been on TV for a long time?" she asked, with a funny little smile on her face. "I don't think I've seen your face before."

Jonah thought for a moment. He had maybe been on

television once, on the news in a crowd scene at Macy's during Christmas. He had standards about lying, and they were simple. He would lie if the story he told wasn't going to hurt anyone and if it might protect him from trouble.

"I don't like any lies," his mother had told him when he explained his rules about lying to her. "They always bring you more trouble."

"I know," Jonah said. "Mostly, I try to tell the truth."

And he did. But sometimes he couldn't help himself.

Jonah leaned over the desk and looked straight at the peach-haired woman.

"I've been on television in New York City," he said.

"No kidding," said the woman, taking a bite of her sweet roll. "You learn something every day."

"Right," Jonah said.

"How old are you, anyway?"

"Eleven," he said. "Twelve in December. I'm probably one of the youngest people on television."

Across the room, *The Mary Hoyer Show* was playing. A small woman with fuzzy yellow hair, who wore a rainbow-colored dress, was interviewing the mayor of New Haven.

"That's Mary Hoyer," the woman at the desk said. "The manager is out sick, but I'll ask her if she'll talk to you at the end of her show."

Jonah sat down to watch.

The show was not interesting. The mayor was talking

about a problem with sewage in the city, and Mary Hoyer's high-pitched voice hurt Jonah's ears.

He would remember that when he started his own show, he told himself. Occasionally his voice sailed up the scale out of the blue and he seemed to squeak instead of talk. But mostly, his mother had told him — his grandmother, too — he had a nice, low, musical voice and maybe should try singing.

At ten, Mary Hoyer's show was over and an exercise program — led by Veronica, in a turquoise bodysuit — came on.

Jonah waited. The peach-haired woman made a phone call. Then she got up from her desk and came back with a plastic foam cup and another sticky bun, smiling at Jonah as she walked by. After fifteen minutes of Veronica, Jonah went over to the desk.

"Did you tell Mary Hoyer I was here?" he asked.

"I did," she said. "Mary has a busy morning."

"Does she think she can see me?"

"Maybe," the woman said, not as friendly as she had been before, even irritated. "She didn't say one way or another."

"Well," Jonah said, a sinking feeling in his stomach, "I have another appointment."

The woman shrugged. "Wait until Veronica finishes, and I'll call Mary's office again."

So Jonah sat down. Other people came into the reception room. A young man wearing blue jeans and a baseball cap turned backward and carrying a fiddle sat down for a moment. He asked Jonah whether he had a breath mint and then disappeared into the back of the studio. A very tall, fluttery woman came in with a suitcase, spoke to the receptionist, and put the suitcase down in the chair next to Jonah's.

By this time Veronica was finished, and the young man in need of a breath mint was on television with his fiddle. A huge stuffed dragon, the size of a small child, sat beside him while he played.

The woman opened the suitcase and took out a white jacket and pants and shoes, and a chef's hat that had *Cooking with Carol* on it. She sat down on the couch and watched the young man with the fiddle.

"I hate this stupid program," she said to no one in particular, unless it was Jonah. "Every week he sits there with that dragon and this foolish expression on his face."

"They're ready for you on the set, Carol," the woman at the desk said.

"Well, I hope they are ready," Carol said, gathering her things and closing the empty suitcase. "Last week there was no vanilla or nutmeg, and the stove was on the blink. It was very difficult to make crème caramel."

"Carol's show comes on next," the peach-haired woman said.

Jonah walked over and stood next to her desk.

"Did you call Mary Hoyer?"

"I will now," she said.

She pressed a few numbers, then spoke again. "Mary, can you see this young man now?" She listened. "I see. Okay, I'll tell him." There was a pause, then she nodded. "I'll tell him to send the tapes."

She put down the receiver and looked up at Jonah. "Mary can't see you today. She said to send in tapes of some sample interviews for your program with a letter describing it, and some tapes from your work in New York City."

"I just had some questions," Jonah said.

"She'll answer them after she's seen some of your work," the woman replied.

"I don't have videotapes, only audio. Is that okay?" Jonah asked.

"That's fine," she said.

"I have another problem," Jonah said. "I don't have a tape recorder anymore. I had to leave mine in New York."

"You're in luck," the peach-haired woman said, coming out from behind her desk. "We keep old tape recorders here. When we get enough of them, we give them away to the public schools."

"So maybe I can use it for the tapes and give it to my school when I finish," Jonah said. "I'm at Bixley."

"Okay by me," the woman said. She opened a box beside her desk, reached in, and handed Jonah the tape recorder that was on top. "And I'll throw in a new tape for good luck."

Jonah opened his book bag, put the tape recorder inside, then zipped it up again. "Thank you very much," he said.

"So — you do the tapes, send us some clips from New York, and who knows? I'm sure you'd be easier to have around than Carol the Cook."

Back on Angel Street, Jonah found an ice-cream shop and ordered a double-decker vanilla swirl and butter pecan. He sat down at a table near the window. It was eleven-thirty. If he took the next bust to Greeley, he would arrive at Bixley right after lunch. He opened his book bag, took out a piece of plain paper from his science notebook, and wrote in his best handwriting:

> *Dear Mr. Parker,*
>
> *Jonah is late today because he had a business appointment at WKBY. Please excuse him. Also he did not finish his homework.*
>
>

Sincerely and best wishes,
Nora Morrison
>

Then he took out the tape recorder and turned it on, pressing the "record" button.

"Testing, testing. This is Jonah Morrison, coming to you from WKBY in Connecticut."

He hit the "play" button.

"Testing, testing." He heard his own voice, and it sounded wonderful. "This is Jonah Morrison, coming to you from WKBY in Connecticut."

■ THE MIDDLE ■

FIVE

Jonah knew he was late for school by the light that spread in a long, pale-yellow rectangle through his window across his blanket, but he kept his eyes closed against the morning.

"Jonah!" his mother called. Jonah could hear the rattling of pots and pans, could smell the coffee brewing. "Jonah, darling, it's nearly seven-thirty. I've got to hustle out of here, and you've got to do the same."

Quentin was complaining in a loud voice, but Jonah could still hear his mother asking whether he was dressed and ready for school, with his books packed and his homework done.

"Almost," Jonah called, still lying on his back in his pajamas, with the covers pulled up over his head. He'd been up for most of the night, practicing.

"Good evening," he'd said into the tape recorder. "This is Jonah Morrison, broadcasting from the Whale. I'm calling to speak with Mr. Michael Jordan. Hello, Michael.

Hello. This is Jonah. You bet. I'm sitting here at my desk in the belly of a whale with some questions for you from the kids of America. Right, kids? Like, first off, where did you learn to play basketball? Where? In your backyard with your daddy?

"I did, too," Jonah went on, sitting up in his bed long after midnight — with the lights out, so his mother would think he was sleeping. "My dad and I played basketball, only I was never any good. He was. Not as good as you, but pretty good. He'd be amazed to know I was talking to Michael Jordan. He'd be very proud of me."

"Jonah!" The door to his bedroom opened, and his mother looked in. "Jonah Morrison."

"I'll be up," Jonah said, hopping out of bed. "I'll be dressed in a second, Mama, I promise."

"What is going on with you, Jonah?" his mother asked quietly. "Are you in some kind of trouble?"

"Nothing, Mama," Jonah said, sliding his tape recorder under the bed with his foot, so she couldn't see it. "No trouble. I've just been thinking a lot."

"Well, you'd better stop thinking quite so much, Jonah," his mother said. "You're going to miss breakfast this morning and you'll have to walk to school eating a bagel along the way."

She put her hands on her hips. "Are you hurrying or not?"

"I'm hurrying," he said. He dressed quickly, and packed

his backpack, slipping the tape recorder in with the books, following his mother, who was carrying Quentin, out of the apartment, down to the sidewalk, and out of the complex to the bus stop.

When his mother got on the bus to go to the day-care center — kissing him good-bye, telling him not to think so much — Jonah dropped the bagel over the fence next to the apartment playground. For the first time in two weeks, since he'd left New York, he was too excited to eat.

On Greeley Street, he heard Blister calling for him to wait. She had had her hair done so it looked like cotton candy, and she was wearing a very short skirt.

"I suppose you're wondering why I'm wearing this," she said. "It's my cheerleading skirt. I'm trying out for the sixth-grade squad."

"It's nice," Jonah said.

He didn't know what else to say, although the skirt wasn't nice. It was too short, and it made Blister — with her white, white legs — look a little like a stork.

"Somebody said you actually played hooky yesterday morning," Blister said, trotting beside Jonah. "Mr. Parker tried to call your mother when he read out the roll and saw you weren't there, even though I said you were at a business appointment. But you don't have a telephone. Right?"

"Right," Jonah said. "Max probably said I was skipping school."

"I guess it was Max," Blister said. "He's like that. Sort of a tattletale type. So were you at a business appointment?"

"I had a note from my mother that said I was at a business appointment."

"Cool," Blister said. "I don't know anybody my age with business appointments. What kind of business?"

"I have a television program," Jonah said. "Do you know what an anchor is?"

Blister shrugged. "I don't think so."

"Well, I'm an anchor. That's the person who runs the program — like, on the news — and asks all the questions when someone is getting interviewed."

"So you really have a program?" Blister asked.

"I really do," Jonah said.

"And what were you doing yesterday?"

"I had a business appointment at Station WKBY," Jonah said.

"That's amazing," Blister said. "I've never known a television star."

"I know," Jonah said modestly. "Most kids haven't."

Blister's friend Anne crossed Greeley to walk to school with them, giving Jonah a funny look.

"Jonah has a television program," Blister said.

"What television program?" Anne asked. "A real one?"

"It's real," Jonah said. "It's not quite ready to show yet, but it's very real."

And he told her about WKBY and the tape recorder and the famous people from all over the United States whose stories he was collecting from *People* magazine and interviewing, and how the interviews were going to be on television everywhere, in every house and every school.

"No kidding?" Blister said.

"That's not true," Anne said. "You're too young. You can't be on television."

"Wrong," Jonah said. "I can be, and I am." He stopped at the wall around Bixley and opened his book bag. "Would you like to listen?" he asked, as he took out the tape recorder.

"To what?" Anne asked.

"To my interview with Michael Jordan," Jonah said.

"I've never heard of him."

"He's a basketball player," Jonah said. "The most famous basketball player in the world."

"Even I've heard of him," Blister said loyally.

Jonah pressed "rewind," and then "play."

"Good evening. This is Jonah Morrison, broadcasting from the Whale."

"From the what?" Anne asked.

"The Whale," Jonah said. "In my program, the office on the set is in the belly of a whale. Get it?"

"No, I don't get it," Anne said.

"Me neither," Blister said.

"Listen to the rest," Jonah said, punching "play" again. "I'm calling to speak with Mr. Michael Jordan. Hello, Michael. Hello. This is Jonah."

"What does Michael say?" Blister asked.

"He doesn't say anything quite yet," Jonah said.

"Because he's wandering around a whale's stomach and can't find the door out," Anne said, shaking her head. "This is really dumb."

"I don't think it's so dumb," Blister said as a group of boys from the Bixley apartment complex walked up the street and stopped to watch. "Jonah's got a TV program. Right, Jonah?"

"I do," Jonah said.

"He's got an interview with Michael Jordan on his tape recorder," Blister said. "Play it, Jonah."

"He can't," Anne said. "We're late for school, and we don't have time to listen."

"I have time," Max said.

But Jonah had already put the tape recorder back in his book bag.

"I'll play it at recess," he said.

"It better be good," Jason said. "It better be Michael Jordan."

"It's good," Jonah said, heading up the steps to school, through the back door, down the long corridor to his locker, Blister just behind him the whole way.

"Is it really Michael Jordan?" she asked as he put his things away in his locker.

"Of course." Jonah's heart was beating too hard, his stomach weak. "It's Michael and me talking."

In homeroom, he sat down at his desk and took out the Huck Finn book, opening it to the middle.

The boy in the seat next to him leaned over to whisper: "So I hear you've got a television show."

Jonah nodded, without looking up — not even when Mr. Parker came into the classroom, dropped his books on his desk, and asked the class to come to order. Jonah stared down while Mr. Parker made the announcements for the day, which included soccer practice and cheerleading tryouts.

"I can't remember why you missed math yesterday, Jonah," Mr. Parker said. "Were you sick in the morning?"

"He wasn't sick," someone blurted from the back row. "He has a television program."

"No kidding," Jason said. "He interviewed Michael Jordan."

"I had a business appointment with WKBY yesterday," Jonah said evenly. "I left a note from my mother on your desk."

When the bell rang for first period, Mr. Parker asked Jonah to speak with him.

"What is this about a television program, Jonah?" Mr. Parker asked.

"I'm beginning this television program about people who have made something of their lives," Jonah said. "It's going to be on WKBY."

"A real program?"

"Yes, sir," Jonah said.

"And have you ever been on television?" Mr. Parker asked.

"Yes, I have. In New York," Jonah said. "But this is the first thing I've done on my own."

"Well, I hope you're not going to have to miss much school," Mr. Parker said. "You're a little behind in math, so you can't afford to be absent."

"Okay," Jonah said. But he was already planning to be absent as much as possible.

In science class there was a quiz on invertebrates — which he flunked, since he hadn't studied for it at all and couldn't answer any of the questions. He was the first to hand in his quiz. While he waited for the rest of the class to finish, he started a letter to Thomas Hale.

Dear Thomas,

It looks like I'm going to get an interview with Michael Jordan, and I thought you'd like that. I remember those clips you have of him from People *and know how much you admire him, and I thought you'd probably like to meet him. So when I talk to him, I'll ask if he'd like to have lunch or something.*

Gotta go. I'm in science class, and the copperhead snake of a teacher is coming down my row of desks to have a word with me. I can tell.

Mama got a new red dress for going out. It's shiny and soft. But she hasn't got anybody to go out with. Quentin's got a cold. On the bus, some lady said he might have pneumonia.

Love from your friend,
Jonah M.

During third period, Blister sat down next to Jonah at the long art table where they had been asked to make blueprints of the insides of their apartments or houses. She was in a bad mood.

"I don't want to do my house," she said. "I wish I lived where I used to live before my father married Trixie."

"So draw that instead," Jonah said.

"I can't remember it. I think it was blue." She took out her pencils and ruler. "So how'd you do on your science quiz?"

"I flunked," Jonah said. "I didn't study, because of the television program."

"Me neither," Blister said. "I was practicing cheerleading at Anne's house, but I probably won't make the squad. Some people don't like me."

Jonah shrugged. "They should."

"They say bad things about me," Blister said, leaning over Jonah's paper, looking at the drawing of his apartment. "They say bad things about you, too."

"So, who cares?" Jonah said.

"I care. I don't like it when people are mean to other people. It gives me nightmares."

Jonah smiled at Blister. She was a funny girl and he liked her.

"I hope you're telling the truth about the television thing," Blister said.

"I am telling the truth," Jonah said.

But while drawing the floor plan of his new apartment, he began to feel ill — a sort of hollow, shaky sense in his stomach, as if a hole had been dug in his middle and was filling up with water, drowning him. It was a strange, sickish feeling and he wanted to go home.

At recess, he went to the infirmary.

"The guys are waiting to hear your tape of Michael Jordan," Blister called as she passed Jonah on her way to cheerleading tryouts. He didn't tell her about the infirmary.

"Right," he called back.

Lying on the bed in the nurse's room, waiting for Aunt Lavinia to pick him up and take him to her house for the afternoon, Jonah closed his eyes. He pretended that Bixley Elementary had disappeared, that he was resting on Aunt Lavinia's couch — or, better still, at his old apartment in the East Village, before Thomas Hale left.

"I need your help," he imagined saying to Thomas Hale.

"What kind of help do you need, Jonah?" Thomas replied.

"I need your help to make up a television program out of those stories you cut out from the magazine."

"Sure, I'll help you out," Thomas Hale said. "Let's start with Michael Jordan. But you've got to get him on the telephone. You can't just pretend."

Jonah Morrison was in over his head. Somehow he had to make *Jonah, the Whale* real, and not just a part of his dreams.

S I X

The day after he had gone to Aunt Lavinia's with the stomach flu, Jonah asked his mother about a telephone.

"We could have one in the kitchen, so we could sit at the table by the window and talk," he said.

"I don't want you calling long-distance to any of your friends back in New York, Jonah. We can't afford it," his mother said.

Jonah looked up from the composition he was writing: "The Most Important Dream of My Life."

"Of course I won't, Mama," he said.

"And I don't want you calling all over the world for Thomas Hale, you hear?"

"Aunt Lavinia says she thinks he's in New York," Jonah said.

"That's as good a place for him to be as any."

His mother was cooking spaghetti sauce, and Quentin was sitting on the floor zooming his little car. Outside, the evening was black and stormy.

"So, tell me about your composition, sweetheart," his mother said. "What is the most important dream of your life?"

"You know what it is," Jonah said.

"No, I don't," she said. "Unless it's that television show you keep talking about to drive me crazy."

"That's right," Jonah said. "That's what it is, if I can ever make it happen."

"Give it up, Jonah. Don't think about it. Think about being a regular boy. You're going to be twelve soon. Think about being a regular twelve-year-old boy in the sixth grade, playing soccer and doing schoolwork and maybe getting some new friends."

"I think about that," Jonah said. "But it doesn't work."

His mother put on water for the spaghetti and sat down at the table.

"Mr. Parker says our compositions are supposed to have a beginning, a middle, and an end," Jonah said.

"That's what stories have," his mother said.

"Well, I know the beginning, and I know the end — but I can't figure out the middle."

Later, as he waited to fall asleep, Jonah thought about the middle. He knew that he wanted to start a television program called *Jonah, the Whale*. That was the beginning. And he knew that the television program would make him famous, and that Thomas Hale would see it and be extremely proud and come to Connecticut and take them back to New York City. That would be the ending. But he didn't know the middle.

Blister had told him that he'd better do something about the show in a hurry.

"The kids in sixth grade are going to think you're a liar," she'd said, walking home with Jonah the day after he was sick.

"It takes a long time to get a television show started," Jonah told her.

"I know," Blister said. "But they don't know that. And they're so terrible to you, it makes me sick."

They were terrible.

On the day that he went to Aunt Lavinia's with the stomach flu, three boys had come to his apartment late — after dark, too late for eleven-year-olds to be on the street.

"We want to see Jonah and listen to his tape of Michael Jordan," Max had said, when his mother answered the bell.

"Well, Jonah's sick. Ask him tomorrow at school," she told them.

"Can we at least listen to the tape?" they'd asked.

"I don't believe you can," his mother said, shutting the door.

Jonah was wide awake, lying in the dark on his bed, his eyes fixed on the ceiling.

"You want to tell me about the tape of Michael Jordan?" she asked, sitting down on the bed beside him.

"Not especially," Jonah said.

"Well, I think you'd better," his mother said.

And so he told her. Not everything. But he told her that he'd gone into his classroom two days earlier, and there on the blackboard someone had written **Bixley Sixth Grade Welcomes Jonah, the Whale.**

"So all of a sudden, I got this idea that I'd make something out of what they called me," Jonah said. "Like all those stories Thomas used to cut out, about people who'd made something of their lives out of nothing."

"You're sweet." His mother shook her head sadly. "I hate it when they're mean to you, darling."

"But if I make *Jonah, the Whale* something important, then I win," he said. "Don't you get it?"

"I get it," his mother said. "But you know very well Thomas used to drive me crazy collecting all those stories. Pipe dreams."

"I'm looking for inspirational stories," Jonah said. "About people who are heroes to kids. Like Michael Jordan."

"And have you been in touch with Michael Jordan?" his mother asked. "Or did you just tell those boys at school that you had an interview with him on tape?"

"Sort of," Jonah said. "Something like that."

"Oh, Jonah. I don't know. You need to hold on tight

to the truth, or you're going to have trouble in your life."

"I might interview Michael, Mama," Jonah said. "You can never say for sure."

For the rest of the week, Jonah came to school with stories. He was flying to Israel for the weekend for a conference on children. He would be absent on Tuesday because he was interviewing the Vice President. He was going to New York on Friday to see the gymnast without any legs perform. Each week he would study the stories in *People* magazine for ideas.

"I can't go anyplace this afternoon," he said one day. "I have an appointment to talk to Tiger."

"Tiger?" Max asked.

"Tiger Woods," Jonah said. "Don't you read the sports page? He's the greatest golfer in the world."

"You don't have an appointment with Tiger Woods," Jason said. "I think you made it up."

"Jonah makes everything up," Max said. "He gets straight A's for lying."

Jonah pretended not to hear.

"Why don't we ever see you on TV?" Max asked.

"You will," Jonah said. "The show isn't ready to air yet."

"I'm so worried," Blister said to Jonah, hopping on the bus with him after school. "Pretty soon, unless this show happens, no one is going to believe a thing you say."

Jonah shrugged. "So?"

"So, you won't have any friends," Blister said.

"I don't have any friends now," Jonah said.

"You have me," Blister said.

"I guess," Jonah said.

"You have me forever." Blister pulled the cord for the bus to stop. "Do you want to come over today?"

"I can't," Jonah said. "I have to take care of Quentin."

"You poor thing," Blister said.

"I don't mind," Jonah said. "I sort of like it."

That night, as Jonah stood at the window of his apartment and watched the children milling in the courtyard of the Bixley Apartment complex, he was filled with a sadness that nearly made him sick.

"Don't you want to go out, Jonah?" his mother asked.

Jonah shook his head. He sat down on the couch with his mother and put his head on her shoulder.

"You're having trouble making friends around here, aren't you?" she asked.

"Maybe," Jonah said.

"I worry," his mother said. "All you seem to do is take care of Quentin and read that *People* magazine and dream about being a TV star. It's not normal."

Jonah stretched out on the couch and watched his mother. She was a pretty woman, he thought, only a little tired from how hard she had to work. It made him un-happy that she didn't have a man to help her out and he didn't want to trouble her. But she seemed in a soft mood for asking favors. And so he asked her once again about the telephone.

"I just wondered whether we could have a telephone," he said. "I think I'd have more friends if we did. I could call them up and talk even when I'm baby-sitting Quentin."

"I guess you could," his mother said.

"I know it costs money."

"I'm doing better now, with these two jobs and tips at the restaurant. So I'll think about the telephone."

Jonah didn't have it in mind to call his friends. He didn't have any friends but Blister, and he didn't need a telephone to talk with her.

He had in mind calling the Vice President of the United States, and the gymnast without any legs, and the Food for All program, and Tiger Woods, and — most especially — Michael Jordan.

"Hello, this is Jonah Morrison of *Jonah, the Whale* call-ing to speak to Michael Jordan. You may not know of my program," he would say, "but I interview inspirational people like Michael for children's television, so that chil-dren everywhere can be inspired by him."

■   ■   ■

When his mother came in to kiss him good night — the night before his composition was due — she asked whether he had finished it yet.

"Not quite," Jonah said. "I'm just lying here, thinking about the middle."

And as he drifted off to sleep, the middle of his dream composition finally began to take form.

SEVEN

The next Monday, the phone company installed a new telephone in the Morrisons' apartment. That afternoon, after Jonah stopped with Quentin at Sweets 'n' Things for a double-dip ice-cream cone to share, he settled down at the kitchen table with the Michael Jordan stories he had collected from *People* magazine. There were three, and one which Jonah particularly liked about when Michael Jordan was a little boy. He opened up his notebook and wrote:

Questions for Michael Jordan

1. How old were you when you started to play basketball?

2. What is the worst thing that happened to you when you were little?

3. Do you have any children or pets?

4. How does it feel to be famous?

5. What do you want to tell the children in America to do to be just like you?

Five questions seemed enough to give Michael Jordan a chance to talk, but not too much.

"I'm going to be making business calls," Jonah said to Quentin, who was sitting on the floor playing with the pots and pans Jonah had taken out of the cupboard for him. "You're going to have to be very quiet so that I can hear Michael Jordan on the phone."

Quentin looked up, smiling. He picked up a saucepan and banged it hard on the linoleum floor.

"Shhh," Jonah said. "You know Michael Jordan, Quentin? He's the most famous basketball player in the world."

Quentin tilted his head.

"Ice cream?" he asked.

"We had ice cream," Jonah said. "What about Cheerios?"

"Cheerios," Quentin said happily.

Jonah poured some Cheerios in a bowl and put it down next to Quentin, among all the pots and pans. Then he sat back at the kitchen table, opened his tape recorder, and checked the tape.

"Promise — no banging. I'm just about to call."

"No banging," Quentin said earnestly.

The article in *People* reported that Michael Jordan lived in Chicago, so Jonah called the operator for the Chicago area code. Once he'd dialed the information operator in Chicago, he asked for the number of the office of the Chicago Bulls — Michael's team. He dialed the number.

"Chicago Bulls," a man's voice answered.

"Hello, this is Jonah Morrison calling from Connecticut. I am the anchor for the children's news program called *Jonah, the Whale.*"

"You've got the offices of the Chicago Bulls," the man said. "We're an NBA team."

"Yes, sir. That's why I'm calling you," Jonah said calmly. "I'm calling to speak with Michael Jordan."

"I'm afraid that's easier said than done, Mr. Morrison," the man began.

"You can call me Jonah."

He explained to the man about *Jonah, the Whale* and how he would be broadcasting his interview with Michael Jordan from an office inside a whale.

"It's sort of a gimmick," Jonah said.

"Run that by me again," the man said.

So Jonah told him about the program and why he wanted Michael Jordan because he was a hero for kids, and he went on to say that he was eleven, turning twelve in December, and had been on television for many years but this was his first solo show. *Jonah, the Whale* was an inspirational show for children.

"We want Michael because he's the number one athlete in the world."

"Well, he's not here," the man said.

"Is he at home?" Jonah asked.

"He may be at home, Mr. Morrison, but I can't give out his telephone number to just anyone. I don't know you."

"Is there any way I can talk to him?" Jonah asked.

"I'll tell you what," the man said. "You give me your number, and the next time I see him, I'll tell him you called."

"Yes, sir," Jonah said, giving the man his new number at the Bixley apartment complex.

"Can you be reached at this number all the time?"

"This is my office," Jonah said.

He certainly didn't want Michael Jordan calling when his mother was at home.

"I'm here from three to seven-thirty on weekdays."

"I'll give Mr. Jordan your number," the man said. "But before you hang up, I have a question for you."

"Yes, sir."

"Are you inside the belly of a whale right now?"

Jonah considered.

"Yes, sir," he said.

"And what's it like in there?" the man asked.

"It's nice," Jonah said. "Spacious. Not too wet or bloody."

The man laughed loudly.

"I'm glad it's not too bloody," he said. "I'll tell Mr. Jordan that. It might please him to talk to someone sitting inside a whale. You never know."

Jonah replaced the receiver. It was four-fifteen and Quentin had fallen asleep on the floor with a fistful of Cheerios locked in his hand. Jonah picked him up and put him in his crib in the corner of their mother's room.

Then he sat at the kitchen table and waited for Michael Jordan. He tried to do his homework, but he couldn't concentrate. He recopied his questions for the interview. He got a glass of milk and made himself a piece of toast, spreading it thick with jam. And then he made himself another. He paced back and forth in the kitchen. When the telephone rang, he had set up the tape recorder to record Michael Jordan and was at the fridge checking for something else to eat.

"Hello. This is *Jonah, the Whale*," he said quickly.

"I beg your pardon?" his mother said.

"Mama," Jonah said.

"Who did you expect was calling?"

"I just didn't know."

"And what do you mean by answering the telephone with 'Jonah, the Whale'?"

Jonah thought for a moment. He certainly wasn't going to tell his mother that he was waiting for a call from Michael Jordan.

"That's what they call me at school," he said. "Sort of since I got fat."

"Well, I don't want them calling you that, you hear?" his mother said. "It's insulting. So, I certainly don't want you calling yourself 'Jonah, the Whale.'"

She told him she'd be running a little late. She was up for a promotion at her restaurant job and had to stay after work to speak with the manager. She asked about Quentin and said there were frozen dinners in the fridge.

"Macaroni and cheese," she said. "I hate to have you take this responsibility for cooking, Jonah, but I tried Aunt Lavinia and she must be at work."

"Never mind, Mama," Jonah said. "That's fine. No problem." He put down the receiver, and no sooner had he put it down than the telephone rang again. He thought twice before answering it "Jonah, the Whale" but then he did. And he was glad he had, because Michael Jordan was on the line!

"I heard about your program, Jonah," Michael Jordan said. "I don't ordinarily take telephone calls like these, but I was intrigued by yours. So, if you have some questions to ask me, I'll be able to give you a few minutes."

"Did you call back because of the whale?" Jonah asked.

"No, I called back because of you," Michael Jordan said. "I think it's very nice that you're doing a program for children on heroes. Children need heroes. I had them."

"Me too," Jonah said, turning up the volume on his tape recorder. "My father was mine."

"My dad was my hero, too," Michael Jordan said. "And he died."

"Mine didn't die, but I don't get to see him," Jonah said. "I haven't seen him since August."

Michael Jordan said he was very sorry to hear that.

Jonah couldn't believe his good luck. His heart was

beating like mad and his face was flushed, but it was easy talking to Michael Jordan — much easier than he had ever imagined.

"I have five questions," Jonah said.

"Shoot," Michael Jordan replied.

"How old were you when you started to play basketball?"

"I was three years old and I played in the town in North Carolina where I lived."

"What is the worst thing that happened to you when you were little?" Jonah asked.

"The worst thing that ever happened to me was when my father died. Even though I wasn't little any longer."

"Do you have any children or pets?"

"I do have children, and I have a goldfish called Marvella."

"How does it feel to be famous?" Jonah asked.

"I love to play basketball and basketball is what made me famous. But I don't think about fame when I'm playing. I think about basketball and winning. That's all. When a child comes up to me and says, 'Are you Michael Jordan?' then I feel a little funny. I am the little boy Mikey from Gastonia with long skinny legs. I don't quite feel like the famous Michael Jordan who plays basketball."

"What do you want to tell the children in America to do to be just like you?" Jonah asked.

"I don't know about being like me," Michael Jordan

said. "But I'm going to tell my child when he's old enough to listen, 'Do your best and be nice to your mama.'"

"Thank you very much, Michael Jordan," Jonah said.

"Thank you, Jonah."

Jonah was so excited that he danced through the kitchen, kicking the chairs over, flying through the corridor into the living room, crashing on the couch, catapulting from the couch to the floor. Then he was on his feet again, back to the kitchen where the telephone was ringing.

"Hello, this is Blister," she said. "I'm calling for Jonah."

"This is Jonah," he said.

"I'm calling to invite you to my birthday party," Blister said. "It's this Saturday."

"Okay," Jonah said. "I'll come."

This day was going better and better. He felt as if he might explode.

"Aren't you going to ask what time it is?"

"Sure," Jonah said. "What time is it?"

"It's at five o'clock at my house, 1213 Raymond Street, and it's a dress-up party with dancing and kissing games and stuff."

Jonah's breath went out of him.

"I've never been to that kind of party," he said.

"It's the first sixth-grade party like this," Blister said. "But you don't have to kiss."

"I don't even know how to dance," Jonah said.

"I'll teach you," Blister said. "Maybe tomorrow I'll come

over to your house, since you have to take care of your little brother."

"Tomorrow I may have to go to my aunt Lavinia's," Jonah said.

"I promise you about the kissing," Blister said matter-of-factly. "You won't have to do it if you don't want to."

Jonah said okay, he wouldn't, and was just hanging up the phone when he heard his mother's key in the door.

She was home earlier than he had expected. She wasn't in a very good mood. Her interview for a better job at the restaurant hadn't gone as well as she had hoped. She wasn't getting a promotion and she was catching a cold.

"How come the interview was bad?" Jonah asked her.

"They just thought I wouldn't have time to do so many jobs and take care of you and Quentin," his mother said, taking out the frozen macaroni. "And they're right. I don't have time."

"We need some more money, don't we?" Jonah asked, setting the table.

"Yes, we do," his mother said. "We're getting by okay, but you need new trousers and I need to have some fillings in my teeth — and if Quentin doesn't get some new clothes, he's going to have to go to day care in nothing."

"Well, maybe I can help," Jonah said.

"Are you thinking of a paper route?" his mother asked. "My brothers had paper routes when they were your age."

"Nope," Jonah said. "I'm not thinking of that."

His mother put the macaroni dinners in the oven and called Aunt Lavinia to tell her about the job, and then she called her mother in New York City and told her that everything was going fine and Jonah had lots of new friends.

"Have you used the telephone much yet?" she asked Jonah as they sat down to dinner.

He was going to tell her about Michael Jordan, but she didn't seem to be in the right mood to hear about long-distance calls or anything else, especially his television program.

"Blister called. My friend Blister, the one I told you about," Jonah said. "I gave her the number today at school."

"Lavinia says she saw Thomas Hale when she was back in New York, but she didn't talk to him," his mother said.

"So maybe he'll call us, now that we have a phone," Jonah said.

"Maybe he will," his mother said quietly.

Later, when he thought about it, Jonah sensed she had seemed sad.

Just before he went to bed, he rewound the tape with his interview with Michael Jordan. Then he pressed "play," turning the volume down.

"Jonah, the Whale," he heard himself say on the tape recorder.

There was silence. "Did you call back because of the whale?" The silence went on and on.

"Me too," his voice came on again. "My father was mine." And once more, his voice was followed by silence. He turned up the volume, but all he could hear was the hollow sound of the tape turning in the recorder without a sound.

"Mine didn't die, but I don't get to see him," his tape-recorded voice said.

Jonah pressed "stop," and buried his head in his hands.

Michael Jordan's voice wasn't on the tape. The sound hadn't registered over the telephone. All that Jonah had recorded was his own voice asking the questions. There was nothing at all of Michael Jordan.

E I G H T

Blister went over to Jonah's after school on Tuesday. It had been her idea. Not even an idea. During science class, she's leaned over the body of a praying mantis pinned to a board for the sixth-grade students to inspect, and said, "I can come over to your house today."

He hadn't even asked.

"Sure," he said. "Today's okay."

"I have nothing to do all week after school, since we ran out of money for me to take ballet," Blister said. She followed him to the library. "I guess you know I didn't make cheerleader."

"I didn't know," Jonah said.

She didn't seem terribly sad — but he could tell, just to look at her, that she was probably brokenhearted.

"Well, I didn't," Blister said. "I wasn't even runner-up."

She told him about the tryouts. How there were twenty-one girls and they all did two cheers in front of the judges. She did "Acka Lacka Ching — Acka Lacka Chow" and "Go, Bixley! Go-go-go!" with a high jump after the first cheer, and the splits after the second cheer, and she was eliminated in the first round of judging.

"I was fourth best," she said. "Maybe third, because nobody else even tried the splits. But the thing is, I don't look good in short skirts."

"Yes, you do," Jonah said. "You look great to me."

After school she went on the bus with Jonah to pick up Quentin at day care, and then they got ice-cream cones at Sweets 'n' Things, plus a pint of banana frozen yogurt.

"So, I canceled my birthday party," she said.

"How come?" Jonah asked.

"No one could come except you," Blister said. "So there was no point."

"I wasn't sure I could come, either," Jonah said.

"You weren't sure about the kissing," Blister said. "You would have come. I know that. You didn't have anything else to do."

"Don't forget, I have the television program," Jonah said, moving over so Blister could sit down next to him on the bus.

"I didn't forget," Blister said. "That's why I wanted to come over today."

Which is how Blister began to persuade Jonah to call Michael Jordan back, and tell him that the tape recorder that he'd used hadn't been good enough to record voices over a telephone.

"I'll call, if you won't," Blister said.

"I won't," Jonah said.

"Then I'll be your associate."

Jonah gave her the telephone number of the Bulls' office in Chicago. When someone answered, Blister said, "Hello, this is Blister, Jonah Morrison's associate at *Jonah, the Whale.*"

"Blister?" the man asked.

"That's correct," she said. "I don't use my last name for personal reasons."

Michael Jordan wasn't there, and the man said he was too busy to give Michael a message. "Don't you know that Michael Jordan is a busy man, with a big reputation?" he asked.

"Of course I know," Blister said sweetly. "That's why I am calling him."

"It won't work," Jonah said, when Blister hung up.

"It'll work," Blister said. "If Michael Jordan did it once, he'll feel terrible that the tape didn't record. I know he will. He's that kind of person."

"You know him?" Jonah asked.

"Well, sort of," Blister said.

"You've met him?" Jonah asked.

"I haven't met him, exactly, but I read these magazines

about famous people and I known things about them. I know things that I don't know about my best friend," she said, sliding into a chair at the kitchen table. "I mean, if I had a best friend."

"I read those magazines, too," Jonah said. "Mostly I read *People.*"

"I read *People,* too. Every week."

"No kidding?" Jonah smiled.

"My mother says it's disgusting for me to read magazines when I should be reading my library books," Blister said. "But I told her that magazines are not dangerous. I could be carrying knives or doing drugs or watching violent videos in the afternoon while she's at work. She should be grateful that all I do is read magazines about famous people."

"I tell my mother that, too," Jonah said. "She especially hates *People,* but my father has a huge collection. That's what he and I do together. We sit at the kitchen table and go through the magazine and cut out the stories about people who've made up their lives. That's how my father likes to think of it."

He opened his folder, turning to the story of the gymnast without any legs.

"Did you see this story?" he asked Blister.

"I did. It's amazing," Blister said. "I wrote her a letter."

"You did *what?*"

"Her name is Tiffany Bass, and she lives in Spokane,

Washington. So I called information there and asked for the number of Mr. and Mrs. Bass and there were two, and I called them both — and Tiffany answered the phone at the second number."

"You're incredibly daring," Jonah said.

"Not really. I was too nervous to talk to her. I don't know why," Blister said. "I guess because there was her picture in the magazine, and there was Tiffany on the telephone — so I just asked for her address and wrote her a letter, and told her she was an inspiration to me."

"Amazing," Jonah said.

"Let's call her," Blister said. "I have her number in my math book."

"What will we say?"

"Ask her five questions, like you asked Michael Jordan."

"But I can't, of course," Jonah said. "The tape recorder doesn't work."

And so, at five o'clock, just when it was getting dark, Jonah and Blister and Quentin ended up at Tapes Unlimited with Greg, a long, skinny, hairy young man in blue jeans hanging low, and a sweatshirt with *I Love You* written in red letters.

"It's an emergency," Jonah said to Greg. "You see, I'm the anchor for a children-to-children television program called *Jonah, the Whale.*"

And he told Greg about the program, about the Whale,

and how Jonah had a desk in the whale's belly. He told him that he had to broadcast a WKBY show about Michael Jordan without Michael Jordan on the tape, because his tape recorder didn't work over the telephone.

"It's a problem," Greg said.

"It's a tragedy," Jonah said, using his grandmother's language for difficult situations.

"It's not a tragedy," Greg said. "But it is a problem."

"We have to go on the air tomorrow," Jonah said. "I've got to get it fixed today. Pronto."

"And who are you?" Greg asked, turning to Blister.

"Blister," Blister said.

"Is that your real name?"

"It's my stage name," Blister said. "I don't use my last name for personal reasons."

"And you're on the television program from an office inside this whale as well."

"Yes, I am," Blister said. "I am Jonah's associate."

"So, is the television station going to pay for this new tape recorder?"

"I haven't had a chance to let them know about the problem," Jonah said. "It's a new emergency."

"Do you have a credit card?"

Jonah shook his head. "I'm underage."

"Me, too," Blister said. "But I don't have a criminal record."

"I'm very glad to hear that," Greg said, and he was beginning to soften, Jonah could tell. "Why should I trust you to take this new recorder — while I'm fixing your old recorder — and bring it back?"

"Because I'm trustworthy," Jonah said.

Greg folded his arms across his chest and looked at Jonah for a very long time.

"The news has to go on, right?" Greg said finally, without a smile. "Well, I'll see what I can do."

Greg disappeared through a door behind the counter. He was gone for a very long time, long enough for Quentin to become cranky and for Blister to go to the deli next door to buy him an apple and some ginger cookies.

When Greg finally returned, he was carrying a different tape recorder: It was larger, with a microphone.

"The tape recorder you gave me will take a couple of weeks to fix," he said. "Besides, you don't have a microphone, and you need one to tape someone's voice over the telephone. So, I'm going to lend you this recorder until yours is fixed. We'll install a microphone for about twenty-five dollars, so you can do your interviews." Greg put the borrowed tape recorder in a shopping bag. "Is there a telephone in the whale's stomach?"

"It hasn't been installed yet, but you can call me at this office," Jonah said, writing down his name and telephone number and address. He thanked Greg very much, saying he was the best engineer he'd met in all of his years on television, and that he'd send him a tape of *Jonah, the Whale*.

■   ■   ■

There were several sixth graders in the courtyard of the Bixley apartment complex when Jonah arrived with Quentin and Blister. Jason was there, throwing a soccer ball in the air and bouncing it on his head or tossing it to Charlie and Max.

"This is great," Blister said, when she saw them. "Just the people I was hoping to see."

"Don't pay attention to them," Jonah said.

"That's not the point. The point is they'll be paying attention to us, especially since I didn't make cheerleader."

"Just say 'hi,' and ignore them. Pretend they don't exist. Pretend we're well-known television personalities and don't have time to be bothered with sixth-grade creeps," Jonah said.

"Which is true," Blister said.

"Sort of," Jonah said, walking to the right of the boys who were leaning against the fence. They seemed restless, and looked them both over.

"So, Jonah," Max called. "You must be going to Blister's birthday party."

"I am," Jonah said. "A lot of people are."

"Like who?" Jason asked.

"Like people from other schools. Friends of Blister's. A couple of guys from the ninth grade," Jonah said.

"Like who?" Max asked.

"You wouldn't know them," Blister said. "They're older."

They opened the door to the Morrisons' apartment.

"Tell us what it's like kissing Blister," Jason yelled to Jonah.

"I hate them," Blister said, following Jonah into the living room.

"They'll be different when we're famous," Jonah said, leading the way. He carried Quentin up the stairs to the second floor and took out his key. When he opened the door, the telephone was ringing.

"It's probably Michael Jordan," Blister said.

"It's probably my aunt Lavinia," Jonah said.

He picked up the receiver. "Jonah, the Whale," he said, in a low, strong voice. "Hello."

It was Michael Jordan.

"I can't believe it," Blister said, lying on the couch in the living room — after the second interview with Michael Jordan, after the tape recorder that they'd borrowed from Tapes Unlimited was tested, and Michael Jordan's voice came through loud and clear.

Jonah was too excited to sit down. He paced back and forth through the living room, into his mother's bedroom, into the kitchen.

"I think it's a sign," he said. "I think it's a sign we're going to make it."

"Who is 'we'?" Blister asked.

Jonah looked at her. "'We' is us. You and me. Jonah Morrison and his associate, Blister."

"Good," Blister said, stretching. "I was hoping for a job. I've run out of things to do."

Later, after Blister had left and his mother had gone to bed because her cold was worse and Quentin was sleeping, Jonah tiptoed into the kitchen and called information for Manhattan.

"Do you have a number for Thomas Hale?" he asked.

"Yes," the operator said. "We have several people with that name. Too many, unless you know his address."

"I don't know his address," Jonah said, his heart falling. He had so many things he wanted to tell Thomas.

Dear Thomas,

I have this great new friend called Blister, and she was named my associate on my new television program today. You'd like her. She's sassy and wears these short short skirts and sometimes purple nail polish and she's very smart.

I have a surprise for you. But I can't give it to you un-less I know where you are.

Love from your friend,
Jonah

■ **THE END** ■

NINE

Jonah couldn't sleep. He tossed and turned, and got up, and went back to bed. The moon was a bright silver plate in the corner of his window, and the wind a constant whirring sound in his ear.

Finally, as the light of morning spilled over the horizon, still very early, before six o'clock, he got up, got dressed, packed his book bag, placed the tape recorder with Michael Jordan's interview on the top, and went out to the living room.

His mother was sitting on the couch — just sitting, staring off into space.

"What are you doing up and dressed before the light of day?" she asked.

He sat on a chair across from her.

"It's already light," he said.

"Barely," his mother said.

"What are you doing up, then?" Jonah asked.

"Pondering."

"Are you feeling better?" he asked quietly, so as not to wake Quentin who was snoring baby snores in the next room.

"My cold is better," she said. "I'm not feeling any better, though. I'm feeling worse."

"How come you're feeling worse?" Jonah asked.

She pulled her legs under her, turned her head away from Jonah so she was looking out the window at the beginning of day, at the fading moon, a shadow in the sky, at the yellow-leaved oak in the distance.

"I miss Thomas," she said simply.

Jonah was silent. He didn't want her to change her mind. He didn't want her to reconsider — to say, as she had been saying for weeks, that she didn't care where Thomas was, or whether she ever saw him again in her life.

But Jonah's heart was leaping for joy.

If his mother missed Thomas Hale, if she was wishing him back, wishing not to live alone, then maybe, with a little luck, she'd go find where he had gone and say he might come on back and try again.

Maybe Thomas would like Springwood and be able to find a job here. Maybe he'd like the apartment, which was larger than the one in the East Village, clean, and sunny. There were no roaches.

His mother got up, went into the kitchen, took out the orange juice, and poured him a glass. She took the cereal down from the cupboard and sliced a banana.

"Raisin toast?" she asked.

"Yes, please," Jonah said.

He was conscious of the way she moved, how slow and thoughtful it was, how unlike herself she seemed — the way she held her head as if it were too heavy to be supported by her slender neck, the way her brown eyes had fallen sad.

"You think you're going to be okay?" he asked, finishing up his breakfast.

"Oh, I'll be fine, darling," his mother said. "By this afternoon, I'll be the same as usual. Bad-tempered, bossy. Don't you worry!" She laughed.

Jonah put on his jacket. "I'm going to school early today," he said. "I'm meeting my friend, Blister."

"That's fine, sweetheart," his mother said. "I'll be home early tonight, so I can pick up Quentin at day care if you want to do something else after school."

Jonah opened the apartment door, thinking how to say what he had to say so that it sounded casual and unimportant.

"And Mama," he began, his voice softer than usual, the words rolling off his tongue. "If you have a mind to find Thomas and tell him to come back, that's okay by me and Quentin, you know."

"And how do you know what Quentin thinks?"

"I just know," Jonah said, and he closed the door.

■   ▓   ■

Blister was waiting for him at the entrance to the apartment complex.

"My mother thought I was crazy, leaving so early," she said. "But she thinks I'm crazy anyway."

They fell in step.

The day was going to be bright and sunny, maybe even warm, with a softness in the air, and the streets were empty of children. There were workers waiting for the early bus downtown, and traffic rushing by to beat the stoplights.

"So we'll be the first ones at school," Blister said. "Usually I'm the last, because I can't decide what to wear."

This morning Blister was wearing a short red skirt, black tights, a black leotard, and bright red nail polish.

"Apple-red," she said, showing Jonah her nails. "What do you think I should wear on television?"

"I haven't thought about it," Jonah said, walking up the front steps to the school. "I think bright colors show up better."

"It looks like no one's here," Blister said, pushing against the front door of the school.

"Somebody has to be here," Jonah said, following her in.

"So what's our plan?" Blister asked.

"Our plan is this," Jonah said, heading down the corridor, past the library and the all-purpose room, past the fifth grade, into their sixth-grade classroom, which was empty.

"First, I want to play the tape on the playground before school starts. As soon as Max gets here with Jason and some of the other guys, you tell them I have the tape. I'll be sort of casually hanging around the basketball net and they'll come over, and I'll say something like, 'Oh yeah, I do happen to have it today.' And then I'll play it."

"Sounds perfect," Blister said.

They left their books for class on their desks and went to the back of the school, where the playground and athletic fields were located — where the children milled around in groups, waiting for the first bell to ring.

It was almost 8:50 when Max arrived with Jason and Charlie.

"So, we hear you've finally got Michael Jordan," Max said.

"Yeah, I do," Jonah said, his arms folded across his chest, his legs apart just so, in a posture he had seen in pictures of Michael Jordan.

"I just happened to bring him with me today, because I've got an appointment at WKBY this afternoon."

"Yeah?" Jason said.

Jonah opened up his book bag and took out the tape recorder, putting it down on the blacktop. Max sat down on the ground beside it. Jason and Charlie crouched next to him, and gradually most of the sixth grade had gathered around.

"He's a TV star," someone said.

"He's brought his interview with Michael Jordan to school," another said.

"Like Michael Jordan's a big deal?" a third voice asked.

"Of course he's a big deal," the first voice said.

"You guys have to be quiet if you're going to hear," Jonah said.

He pressed the "play" button.

"Hello," the tape began. "I am Jonah Morrison, your host of the first network children-to-children program, *Jonah, the Whale,* coming to you today and every day from the belly of the whale.

"I am sitting in my office in that belly, at a swivel chair in front of a large desk, and today you are going to hear my interview with the one, the only, Michael Jordan.

"First, before we speak to Michael, let me tell you about the purpose of *Jonah, the Whale.*"

There was a long pause, then a cough. In the distance, Quentin was babbling quietly.

"It is our intention here at Station WKBY to bring heroes into the lives of children, people who have invented their lives from nothing, people who are inspirations to others. *Jonah, the Whale* is a program by children and for children. Thank you very much. And now for Michael Jordan, coming right up."

Jonah looked up.

He saw Max lean into Jason. Charlie stared the other way, toward the playground. Some of the children were laughing, but no one said anything about the name.

Jonah, the Whale.

Except Blister, who couldn't help herself.

"So you know where Jonah got the name for the program?" she asked.

"Nope," one boy said. "Maybe the Bible?"

"Remember?" Blister said. "You remember, Max."

Max looked stricken.

"Yes," replied one sixth-grade girl with a high, soft voice. "I remember."

Jonah punched "play" again.

"How old were you when you started to play basketball?" Jonah was saying over the tape recorder.

"I was three. Three years old, and I played across the street on asphalt in my hometown," Michael Jordan was saying.

The group around Jonah was quiet. When the bell rang for the beginning of school, no one moved. Jonah punched "stop," and as the bell stopped ringing, he pressed "play" again.

"I can't believe it," Max said. "How did you get to him?"

"I did the interview by telephone," Jonah said.

"And he answered your call?" Jason asked.

"I left a message at the Bulls' office, and he called me back," Jonah said.

"He called you back at your own telephone number?"

"That's right," Jonah said.

"Amazing."

They all gathered their book bags and fell into step with Jonah and Blister, walking in the back door of the school.

"Jonah's got an interview with Michael Jordan," Max said to Mr. Parker as they walked into the sixth-grade classroom.

"No kidding, Jonah," Mr. Parker said.

"It's for his TV program," Jason said. "Play it for him, Jonah."

So Jonah did. He stood at the front of the class and played the tape, and everybody cheered.

"So, how are we going to get on television now?" Blister asked in science class.

"I'm going to send the tapes to Mary Hoyer at WKBY," Jonah said. "She asked me to send them once I had a few interviews."

"That means we should call Tiffany Bass, the gymnast."

"Right," Jonah said. "We'll call her today after school."

"I want to be the one to talk to her," Blister said.

"You can be the one," Jonah agreed.

■　　■　　■

Jonah went to Blister's house.

"No one's home until seven, when my mother comes in," Blister said. "So we can call a lot of people."

And they did.

First they talked to Tiffany Bass — Blister on the phone in the kitchen, Jonah on the phone in the bedroom. Tiffany spoke very carefully in a small voice.

"I simply decided I wanted to be a gymnast, even though my legs don't work," Tiffany said.

"You're amazing. I can't believe it," Jonah said. "Do you have anything you'd like to say to children all over America?"

"I don't know what to say," Tiffany said. "Maybe they don't want to be gymnasts. But I did — so I am."

The name of the boy who started the Food for All program was Benjamin Kahn. He was at home, packing the van from which the food was delivered every night. He was glad to talk to them.

"People just come to my house and bring food, mainly sandwiches and drinks, and we put it in the back of the van. Then we drive around the streets, passing out food to the homeless until it's gone. And then I do my homework."

"Are you friends with the people to whom you give food?" Blister asked.

"Not particularly. They're glad to see me, but they don't

want to be friends," Benjamin said. "Mainly, my friends are at school."

"Do you have anything inspirational to say to the children of America?"

"Well, peanut-butter sandwiches are the best for people who are homeless, because they fill you up."

"I mean, like, inspirational," Blister said.

"I did this because I wanted to," Benjamin said. "It's very fun."

The Vice President was not available, although someone answered at the White House and said, "White House." They could not find a number for Stevie Wonder. But, by seven o'clock — when Jonah had to go home — they had their three tapes and had written a letter to Mary Hoyer at WKBY.

Leaving Blister's apartment to go home, Jonah was pensive.

"I think if this works out, I'm going to tell the truth always," he said. "Do you remember when I told you about my sister?"

"I remember. You have a married sister," Blister said.

"But I don't really have one," Jonah said. "I made it up — because you have a married sister, and I wanted to have the same as you."

Blister's lips turned in a half curl at the side of her

mouth, and she was smiling, a small, embarrassed smile.

"I don't have a married sister, either," she said. "I don't have any sisters at all. But I'd like to have one."

"No wonder we're best friends," Jonah said.

"No wonder," Blister agreed.

TEN

The inside of the whale was dark pink with occasional splashes of gray paint and was made of material that appeared soft, although the floor of the belly was wood and painted pink. Jonah's desk was in the middle, a small desk piled with papers, on which there was a telephone. There was a couch for Jonah's guests, as well as a large comfortable chair on which he and sometimes Blister could sit to interview guests.

On the first of December, Jonah and Blister had been dismissed early from school, since it was the first of the series of *Jonah, the Whale.* The show aired at five o'clock every Monday afternoon and would run for thirteen weeks.

"Just for today, you can leave early," Mr. Parker said, "to be sure that everything is ready for the show."

So, after lunch, Jonah and Blister packed their book bags, took the suitcase with the outfits they planned to wear for their first television appearance, and headed out the front door of Bixley Elementary, where Aunt Lavinia was waiting to drive them to WKBY.

Everybody in the sixth grade followed them. Max threw his arm around Jonah's shoulder, Jason pushed in close, Charlie and Andrew and Bruce and Frankie and Sleako and Bo and Dick, all the boys in sixth grade that Jonah hardly knew, who had never really spoken to him as if they hadn't even known he existed, were at the front of the school, hoping to be chosen as Jonah's friend. And Blister was surrounded by high-spirited girls who danced around her, screaming "Good luck!" and "Wave to me on camera," and "Say 'Hi, Anne!'"

Jonah climbed into the front seat of Aunt Lavinia's car and Blister got in the back. They both waved as the car pulled away from the curb and turned right on Greeley.

"I guess you're pretty popular," Aunt Lavinia said.

"I guess," Jonah said. "I'm pretty nervous. I know that."

"I'm not at all nervous," Blister said. "I have a bright red skirt and a white blouse and black tights, and my mother says I should wear my hair brushed out sort of like a fuzz-ball."

"What are you wearing, Jonah?" Aunt Lavinia asked.

"Just blue jeans," Jonah said. "And a red shirt. I'll wear the same thing every Monday. A sort of uniform."

"You're going to have to wear lipstick," Blister said. "Everybody does on television."

"Wrong," Jonah said. "I'm in charge of what happens today."

Jonah Morrison was in charge of everything that was going to happen from five to five-thirty at WKBY on this Monday afternoon, December 1. He had worked very hard for this day and now that it was here, he could hardly believe his good fortune.

"We'll give you a trial run," Mary Hoyer had said. "And if you have a lot of children who are watching *Jonah, the Whale,* then we'll make you a regular."

Michael Jordan had agreed to be the first guest. Not in person. He couldn't get away from Chicago on the first of December. But he was going to be interviewed by satellite, with his image flashed onto a big screen, as if he were there in person.

"Don't worry, Jonah," Michael said. "I'll see you sitting there in the middle of that whale, and you'll see me on a screen right in front of you, so it will seem as if we're there together."

"It would be nice if Thomas knew I was going to be on TV," Jonah said as Aunt Lavinia pulled up in front of the television studio. "Michael Jordan is his favorite."

"Maybe he knows, Jonah. Someone might have shown him the story in the paper last week."

"I don't think he'd see something like that," Jonah said, climbing out of the car. "Not if he still lives in New York."

"Well, I'm going to pick up your mama and Quentin, and we're both going to my house to watch you."

"I told her I didn't want her at the studio," Jonah said. "It makes me too nervous."

"Makes her pretty nervous, too, sweetheart," Aunt Lavinia said.

"I'm think I'm getting sick," Blister said to Jonah, hopping from the car onto the sidewalk.

"You can't, Blister," Jonah said. "This is your chance to be somebody, and you can't blow it."

"You can't, either," Blister said.

"I'm not going to blow it," Jonah said.

The music started first and then came the image of a whale, a particularly fat whale. Across its broad body, letter by letter, rolled the words J-o-n-a-h, t-h-e W-h-a-l-e.

Jonah, sitting at his desk, with Blister beside him, took a deep breath.

He heard the sound engineer say, "10–9–8–7–6–5–4–3–2–1. You're on."

"Welcome to *Jonah, the Whale.* I'm Jonah Morrison, your host of the first children-to-children program, coming to you today, and every Monday for the next thirteen weeks, from the belly of a whale called Jonah, named for me. And this is my associate, Blister. Our job, as kids just like you guys sitting in front of your television, is to bring heroes into your houses, people who have invented their lives from nothing, who are an inspiration to others.

"Today we're lucky enough to be talking with the greatest basketball player in the world, a man so good that he'll melt your heart — Michael Jordan. Hey, Michael. Welcome to *Jonah, the Whale*."

"Hey, Jonah," Michael Jordan said, bigger than life. "How're you doing, Blister? And the rest of you kids in Connecticut. I'm glad to be here, to talk to all of you sitting at home. I hope you have a good snack."

Everyone from the studio was cheering when the music played at the end of the program as the lights went down and Jonah walked off the set with Blister.

"It was amazing," they said. "Michael Jordan was wonderful!" "You were wonderful!"

"I almost threw up," Blister said.

"But you didn't," Jonah told her, nearly shaking with excitement.

When they left the studio at six o'clock, Aunt Lavinia was waiting outside for them.

"I didn't think you ought to come home on the bus," Aunt Lavinia said. "Not celebrities, like you two kids."

"So, did you like it?" Blister asked.

"Like it?" Aunt Lavinia said. "It was extraordinary, Jonah. We are proud to bursting, your mama and I. And Quentin licked the television screen when he saw your faces."

"It was fun," Jonah said. "I didn't think it would be."

"So who's on next week?"

"Tiffany Bass," Blister said.

"She's flying here to be interviewed in person," Jonah said. "She's going to do a performance on the set."

"So, sweetheart, are we going to stop for one of your double-dip ice creams on the way home?" Aunt Lavinia asked.

"We're not hungry," Blister said. "Are we?" she asked Jonah.

"Nope," Jonah said. "Let's go home."

They drove up to the apartment complex. Even though it was beginning to rain and the night was already black with only a whisper of light in the sky, the courtyard was full of children. They screamed as Jonah and Blister got out of Aunt Lavinia's car.

"Like we're rock stars," Blister said.

"I don't want to be a rock star," Jonah said. "All I've been wanting to be, ever since I came here, is just an ordinary kid."

"Well, you're that now, too," Blister said, walking with

him through the crowd to Jonah's apartment. His mother stood at the entry door with Quentin.

"I've invited your friends over for hot chocolate and cookies, darling," his mother said, stepping aside while everyone rushed by up the stairs to the apartment. "They've been wanting to see you."

She hugged him tightly, and Quentin wrapped his chubby arms around Blister's neck.

The telephone was ringing when Jonah walked into the apartment, which was splendid with balloons and streamers and the sweet smell of hot chocolate. He ran to answer it.

"Hello," said the familiar voice on the other end. "I'm calling to speak to Jonah Morrison of *Jonah, the Whale.*"

Jonah sat down on the kitchen chair, his blood suddenly thin, his breath shallow, his heart expanding beyond the limits of his chest.

"You've got Jonah Morrison on the phone," he said to Thomas Hale. "How come you knew about my show?"

"Your aunt Lavinia found me and sent me the notice about it from the paper," Thomas said. "I am impressed, Jonah."

"Thank you, Thomas," Jonah said. "I guess the idea was sort of yours in the first place."

"From our *People* magazine clips?" Thomas asked.

"Right," Jonah said, suddenly embarrassed. He put his

hand over the receiver, motioning to his mother. "You prob-ably want to speak to Mama."

"I would like to speak to your mother," Thomas said.

"It's for you," Jonah said as she made her way through the crowd of children to the telephone.

"Who is it?" she asked.

"Somebody you know," Jonah told her, trying not to smile.

Later, Blister and Jonah lay in the dark on the floor in the living room, their feet up on the wall, watching the yellow headlights from the passing cars paint stripes across their arms and faces.

"If I wanted, I could be a cheerleader now," Blister said.

"I guess you could be," Jonah said.

"But I don't want to be," Blister said.

"You'll be too busy to practice," Jonah said. He was thinking about Thomas, who was coming to Spring-wood, coming home. In the kitchen after dinner, wash-ing up the dishes, his mother had told him what had happened.

"He left because he felt bad."

"Bad about what?" Jonah asked.

"He didn't have a good job, and we could only afford an apartment with lots of roaches," his mother said.

"I thought it was my fault," Jonah said.

"Your fault?" his mother asked. "Now, why would you think a thing like that?"

"I just did," Jonah said.

"Well, you weren't responsible," his mother said. "Thomas was, and so was I, but you had nothing to do with the trouble we've had."

"And you're glad that Thomas is coming back?" Jonah asked.

"Are you crazy?" His mother laughed one of her loud belly laughs and hugged him hard. "You bet I'm glad!"

"Are you listening, Jonah?" Blister got up on her elbow and turned to him. "Do you think someone is going to make a movie about us?" she asked.

"I don't think so," Jonah said. "But we could be in *People* magazine before school's out."

"Maybe on the cover," Blister said happily. "I think I'll wear that shiny turquoise skirt I found in the trash bin and teeny-tiny high heels and lip gloss for the picture."

Jonah closed his eyes and imagined the cover of *People* magazine. He was sitting at his desk in the belly of the whale and Blister was standing beside him in her shiny turquoise skirt. Across the front of the cover, in bold red letters, were the lines: *Young kids come out of nowhere to become really, really famous.*

A noisy truck with enormous headlights stopped just outside the Bixley Apartments, flooding the living room where Jonah and Blister were talking, and suddenly they were both lit up bright yellow in the darkness.

"The television crew has their spotlights on us," Blister said.

"Tell them we're busy," Jonah said. "They need to make an appointment."

About this Scholastic Signature author

SUSAN SHREVE is the author of several acclaimed books for children, including *The Goalie, The Gift of the Girl Who Couldn't Hear,* and *The Flunking of Joshua T. Bates,* and is a professor of English at George Mason University.

Ms. Shreve has four almost-grown children and lives in Washington, D.C.